The Beginnings of Infinity

The Beginnings of Infinity

Ethan Reyna

Copyright © 2017 by Ethan Reyna.

ISBN:	Softcover	978-1-5434-1274-1
	eBook	978-1-5434-1273-4

All rights reserved. No part of this book may be reproduced or transmitted in any form or by any means, electronic or mechanical, including photocopying, recording, or by any information storage and retrieval system, without permission in writing from the copyright owner.

This is a work of fiction. Names, characters, places and incidents either are the product of the author's imagination or are used fictitiously, and any resemblance to any actual persons, living or dead, events, or locales is entirely coincidental.

Print information available on the last page.

Rev. date: 03/30/2017

To order additional copies of this book, contact:
Xlibris
1-888-795-4274
www.Xlibris.com
Orders@Xlibris.com
755727

Dedicated to Time,

for always moving in a positive

direction and growing my mind.

Chapter I

I shall begin at the beginning. Of all of the places in between that and infinity, the beginning seems to be the best to start with. You, reader, believe there was a "big bang". But your "human" race knows very little of the world around them. For example, you also still believe that there is no cure for cancer. A cellular mutation that has killed more of your kind that all of your wars combined. It's a shame really. So, the beginning, well my beginning is very clear to me for those of my same universal race and I live infinitely long lives compared to that of a human. Though they lack the capacity to understand it; one true fact that humans have figured out is the theory of things being infinite. But when a human thinks of infinity, they think of a tree of time branching off from their current location, forwards. This is the part that they don't understand. Infinity runs both ways. BACKWARDS as well as forwards. We only exist in the middle of an infinite web of possibilities within an infinite number of infinite webs of possibilities. Therefore there is NO beginning! Just like how there is no end. Infinity is infinite. Imagine that.

When I popped into existence I was but a figment of my own imagination. I was smaller than an electron and with no form. I don't remember seeing very much for the first hundred centuries. During which time I was very lonely. I didn't feel the collision of another single being until I was at least five (500 centuries human time). It was a pretty little photon of red light. So sweet and calm. She was so slow and groggy in her movements but was just as glad to see another's existence as I was.

As we collided, the conversation went as follows. (Collision) "Oh! Hello there!" I said. "Salutations," she said in a melancholy tone. As if she was tired after a long journey. "What is your name?" I asked in a truly sincere way. "Red," she said. I thought this to be a rather strange name but I couldn't complain because I, myself, didn't have a name yet. Red asked me my name and I gave her nothing but mystery. "Do you not have a name young one?" she asked. "No," I replied sadly, "I am only five hundred centuries old and I don't even know where I came from or how I came about." "That is unfortunate," she said, "you must think, the universe is so very big, but we overcame its vast emptiness by meeting each other. That is something we do know." I have yet to meet an existing being that spoke truer words than Red.

"Do you know where you came from?" I enquired of her. "Yes! I remember it very well!" she answered, "Would you like me to share the tale with you?" "Oh yes please!" "Very well. Come closer so that we can see each other to the best of our ability." She said, and so I did. "It all began with the beginnings of an uprising that I and many of my fellow photons started against the super massive dead star that held us in with its warping of the plane of space." "What is a star?" I asked. "I'll get to that later." She said in a rather inpatient sort of way. She resumed by saying, "The super massive dead star, or Dark as we called him, warped the plane of space so that us photons would be forced up close to his huge body and OH! How Darks stink," she groaned. "Stink?" I asked. "Later," she answered quickly. "So, naturally us photons do not like being so close to Darks because they smell worse than dark matter and they only use us as a type of invisibility cloak so as to sneak up on their smaller, younger neighbors and feast on their very mass!" I jumped back in shock at this horrifying sentence that she spoke.

"Yes, tell me about it! We photons began to come up with ideas about how we could escape the warp that the Dark was creating, for we all were getting very fed up with his revolting musk. So we remembered an ancient tale of a group of photons that banded together to kill the most massive Dark the universe had ever seen. He called himself Hate." My eyes began to widen as she continued into the juicy body of the story. "What our ancestors did is they combined into what is called a singular massive photon, or Soul as we call it, and devoured Hate. But, the only negative was that the photons in the nucleus of the Soul were cast out in all directions when the spirit of Hate was released, and were never seen again." "This is a most wonderful story Red," I said in absolute amazement. "Thank you, but I haven't even gotten to the good part yet." I nearly lost a microgram when she said this. "Then don't stop now!" I said. "Fine, fine, fine! So naturally being me, I didn't want to damn my fellow photons to eternity of loneliness, so I volunteered to be one that was in the nucleus. Plus, I always dreamed of traveling. So we huddled together into the most beautiful and harmonious Soul that there ever was and we devoured that disgusting Dark, which tasted as rank as it smelled, and I was cast through space at ten times my normal speed, until after many long millennia I met the prettiest little thing I ever had seen." "Who was it?" I asked, thinking that she was still telling the story. "You silly!!!" I smiled and embraced her and she smiled and embraced me in return. "That was a lovely story," I complimented. "Thank you. OH! I have a name for you my darling! I have always thought that Love was a beautiful name. I made it up and I think it fits you very nicely." she said. "Love." I repeated. "Do you like it?" she asked. "It is a better name than I could have ever asked for!" I answered.

And so began my life of learning. Red took me places that both of us had never been and showed me things that twisted my nucleus more than anything that I had ever seen. She was like a mother to me. She taught me everything that she knew about the universe and its inhabitants. But everything changed when we exited the dark obis that was my birth place and approached a nebula. The first that I had ever observed.

Chapter II

My sight was strained a great deal as we came within three hundred light years of the cloud. Its glowing hot hydrogen shot Red's clones in all directions and I was introduced to almost all of them. By this time I had grown to the size of a dwarf planet. It had been a total of one hundred thousand centuries (10 years in my time) since my first memories, and five hundred centuries since I had met Red. The size of the nebula began to grow as we approached. After a century of travel it had grown to over five times its initially observed size. But before the other two centuries had gone by something very peculiar happened within the cloud of gas and dust.

We were told by all of Red's traveling clones that the cloud was collapsing. This statement left me very disappointed because I was beyond exited to feel the touch of hydrogen atoms. I turned to Red and asked, "Why is the nebula collapsing?" "Well," she said with a deep breath, "I have heard it said that nebula sometimes collapse in on themselves in order to create something new." I turned back to face the nebula and asked, "But why would it give up all of its beauty to create something new?" "Because that is what it feels is its purpose I assume," she replied.

I looked with a deep admiration as I witnessed the nebula twist and shrink into a spherical shape. It would pulse and puff in and out; almost like when you are about to sneeze and the intensifying feeling is building up. You take several deep breaths in until the ritual is completed by the flinging of air and germs. Instead of a giant nebula sneeze there was an explosion of light. Light that I had never seen before. I saw pure white light. Later, Red explained that that was the birthing of her clones, for that flash contained every color of light there has ever been. It hurt my sense of vision so badly, since I had only been used to Red's soft, dark glow, that I quickly turned away until I could get used to it. Once I had the strength to gaze at it directly it was much more beautiful than I had imagined.

Suspended in the center of a cloud that glowed a beautiful red, a star smiled for the first time and illuminated the universe. With his smile, he dispersed blue light that greeted us as long lost family. At that moment there was an unveiling of the universe as stars began to increase in numbers all around us. Imagine being inside of a bag of microwave popcorn. All around you there would be explosions that left shining white puffs of fluff. What we saw was comparable to that except with bright colorful explosions that left pin holes in the blackness that was the universe.

"What is going on?" I asked Red in a confused and slightly scared tone. "We have entered an active zone in the universe," she replied. "I have never even imagined anything like that happening." "I have only heard of stories," Red said. "Well now we can be the ones that tell the stories," I countered. "Let us explore this active zone and see what we find." More stars were born in the distance as we traveled on.

We encountered many strange objects during our travel of the zone. There were fields of tiny, flying particles called Grins that only lived for a second and then fizzled away. But it seemed that every Grin that was born would touch my very essence, then would leave me with one of the best feelings there ever was. Red told me that the feeling was called Hope. Hope was an entity that only longed to help others get through their lives without ever meeting Fear or Worry, two of the creators of Sadness. Hope ripped himself into an infinite number of pieces to create Grins in order to spread himself to everything in the universe. Every time a Grin was born and died, a piece of the essence of Hope attached to a ray of light hit the viewer, killing any particle of negativity. It was so beautiful to hear such a story be told. Pure sacrifice for the betterment of the universe. I felt a connection with hope and I couldn't explain why.

Red could tell by the way I was suspended that I was in deep thought about the story she had told me. She enquired, "Is there something that you feel from the story that I have shared?" "I feel some kind of connection to Hope. Almost like I know him personally," I answered. She looked at me and said, "I knew it! You are the chosen one. The greatest and most powerful emotion that has ever been made." I puzzled more after she said this because I didn't feel like a chosen one. I just felt like a being that had no idea how he came about and was named by a photon of red light. "There is a prophesy that has been told among photons about the return of the Dark named Hate only with much more size and strength. It is said that he will be more powerful than any soul that can be created, therefor, the most sincere and pure emotion will be born to defeat him. He will be the kin of Faith, Hope, and Happiness and kith to Fear, Worry, and Sadness. That is you my sweet Love." I didn't know what to say. So I just remained silent until I could comprehend what has just told to me. No matter how I tried it was rather difficult to believe.

Red told me that we had to begin our search for the old wise creator that was a being of the greatest knowledge and patience. He could be found at the heart of the universe. So we started yet another journey, but this time it was to the center of the universe, where it is oldest and therefor most dangerous.

Chapter III

As we floated through the speckled void, I began to notice that the atoms of the universe were changing. It seemed as though the molecules themselves were becoming lonesome. Therefore they began to attach themselves to other molecules which in turn created a whole new universe. I met a curious little compound, one day, while Red and I traveled through the tail of a space explorer named Comet. I knew his name because Red could speak his language and was able to introduce us in his native dialect. His language confused me a great deal. To me it only sounded like a mix of whispered consonants with the occasional stress on a strategically placed vowel. As the Comet said goodbye to us and sped across our path, we met the molecule.

"Good day!" I said for it was a bit bright where we were because of a nearby star. "Oh hello there. Did you fall off of that flying rock that always seems to be in a hurry too?" They asked. "Oh no, not I. I am called Love and this is my very best friend in the entire infinity,

Red. We come from a very long way away," I replied. "As do we! In fact we have traveled the diameter of the entire universe it feels." They replied. I was a bit confused when they called themselves "we". Out of confusion and lack of understanding I asked, "you call yourself 'we' but I can only observe one of you, why is this?" they replied as if they were offended that I made the mistake by saying, "What a silly question! Tell us, have you ever seen another molecule like us before in your life?" "Well, to be honest, no," I said in embarrassment. "The reason for that is because we were so lonesome alone we decided to clump together," They said. "What are you each called?" I asked. They spoke separately for a moment when they said their names. (First little voice) "I am called hydrogen," the voice said, "and we are twins and we are both called oxygen," said a second voice that seemed to have two pitches. I was surprised to learn that there were not only two but three molecules in this single compound. I got closer to observe the tiny beings in their entirety.

As I took a closer look I saw them! They were all huddled together in the most beautiful little embrace that I have ever known. I was so overwhelmed to see such beauty being shared between being so I shed a single tear of happiness. The compound looked concerned, so they wiped my tear and asked what was wrong. At the moment that my tear of joy touched their electrons they felt something no one had ever felt before. They felt Love. They changed at that very second into something new altogether. They all collapsed into one under the feeling of the love I had given them and were reborn right before my eyes as water.

They gazed at me in a feeling of completion and thanked me for helping them love each other. I smiled and embraced them and sent them on their own way. I have not and will not forget the first time I shared myself with another being. I cry even now just from telling you about it.

Red and I continued on our path. We talked a great deal about the wonders of the universe. I asked a lot of questions and she gave answers to those that she knew the answers to. Red was always full of answers. It was a rare occurrence that she did not know the answer to a question that I asked. During one of the rare occurrences I asked a rather interesting question. "What is the reason for all of this?" was the question that was uttered and silence followed. Red truly did not know the answer, but Red had a way of giving me at least some kind of answer that way the question didn't trouble me. She answered my question with more of the same. "Why is there pain? Why is there pleasure? Why are we us? Why are they them? The world is full of questions Love. If we aren't careful about what we question, our very existence will be up for debate." Red's advice resonated between my auditory organs. To tell you the truth it warped my noodle a great deal. So I took her advice because I could seem to think anymore.

Many more centuries went by as we continued to meet new creatures and compounds. The combination of molecules seemed to have me end. There were mixtures of compounds and elements that created even more complex compounds. We began to travel through a section of space that humans named the horse head nebula. It turns out that there are a certain group or creatures that call this nebula home. They are called Steeds. They are a rather useless bunch that just chase each other around their planet looking to reproduce. I felt they lacked something very important so I pushed out a quick rain of tears on their planet which made them love each other and only mate with one other their entire lives. Red and I continued on our journey.

Chapter IV

Oh how tiresome the next several hundred centuries were. Not only for me but also Red. We travelled what seemed like forever, and we hadn't even made it to the wise man yet. We came into contact with many different species of life during this time span. At each dwelling I poured myself into it so that their species would have Love, which made me even more exhausted. Because I was so weary I asked Red if we could rest on a planet that was close by, and she agreed.

The planet which was host to our resting was a quaint little satellite of an average solar system. This solar system was one which held a medium sized star. The planet was suspended at just the right distance from its star that the existence of an old friend named water was of very high population. This was my first encounter with your planet. Out of anywhere in the entire universe to feel tired and in need of rest, I ended up in your galaxy. I ended up in your solar system. I ended up on your planet. Now tell me, what other mystery of the universe is greater pondered than that of coincidence? Is that, in fact, what it should be called? Coincidence or fait?

Red and I decreased our speed greatly because we were afraid that your delicate little planet would be completely and utterly destroyed if we arrived at too high of a speed. We descended through the white, clouds of water molecules. I felt it and knew that wherever it was that we had travelled was so beautiful, and completely perfect that I would instantly begin to shed tears, but I contained myself for a little longer. As we traveled farther down, the clouds gave way to a sanctuary for oxygen. They were so absolutely content with each other and their environment. We passed through their dwelling and continued down to the surface. We must have heard and said excuse me five billion times between the clouds and the surface. Never the less, we made it to the surface without a problem and then began exploring.

On Earth there were an innumerable amount of creatures dwelling on this delicate little inflated balloon of water, soil, and air. I tried to talk with each and every one of them, but they just left me with silence. Feeling puzzled, I asked more questions to more creatures and received the same reaction. I began to run around trying to communicate but the creatures didn't even look at me. I was so over whelmed with confusion and the mere stress of, essentially, being a ghost with no one to talk to, that I caught myself beginning to cry. I felt something that was a mystery to me. I felt tears of sadness and worry. I was sad because I couldn't communicate with the creatures despite my full efforts, and I was worried that I was going insane because every time I had ever talked to someone or something, I would get a response. I contained myself for a bit longer due to the fact that I remembered that Red was right next to me the whole time to comfort me.

I turned to Red and said in a chocked voice, "This planet is beautiful even though it has no talking creatures on it." "Maybe it's not that they can't talk. Maybe it's that they can't hear you, and, therefore, cannot respond to that which does not exist in their view of their existence." Red said reassuringly. "Well," I said with a sigh and a sniff, "I want to give these creatures the feeling of Love due to the fact that it could be the only thing keeping this planet together, I doubt very much that it would be put to use here, but I will give it, non the less, in hopes that a certain lifeform will evolve which will put my tears to good use." Red smiled and said, "What a splendid idea."

I let my tears build for so long that when I let them go, it became a rain over the whole planet. It was very similar to a gentle shower that you would see in the spring. I didn't expect to shed that many tears so I stopped as fast as I could. Some of my tears were absorbed by the creatures, but most was drunk by the soil. I thought this to be odd, so I continued to watch. All of the sudden, I saw the planet come alive. I had given Love to the planet itself. The soil became bulging with sustenance which provided food for all of the creatures. I thought to myself, "a species is sure to come along that will inherit this Love from its mother, the planet, and take it for granted. So much so, as to be completely blind to it to give way to selfish thoughts and chaos." I had never wanted anything more but to be wrong at that moment. Today I curse my natural gift of prediction. Life seems to be so much simpler and care free being as blind as a human.

I continued to watch the Love of the planet Earth for her children that she provided for. She gave and gave without a sing desire for anything in return. Pure beauty I the only way that I can describe it. Red and I ascended into the clouds as we resumed our journey. A few hundred more centuries and we had arrived near to our destination.

Chapter V

I have found that one of my favorite things that humans have created is poetry. Though it has no practical use anywhere else but on Earth, I enjoy it none the less. Here is one of my own creation that I used to recite for Red.

> We travel quickly forward into the void of space
> But we begin to slow as dust meets my face.
> So I stop and gaze at the stars that surround
> In awe at their beauty for all have been found
> To be so perfect in my loving eye
> For when I see them I can only sigh
> As I shed a tear and give my Love
> So that infinity will know that I am above.
> I give myself to the solar flow
> To be carried to a heart that is feeling low
> In order to save all that exists

From the nasty taste of a Darks filthy kiss.

Well if my memory is still true I believe those are the right words. Anyway, back to the story. Where was I? Ah yes, Red and I were on our way to the central universe to meet the wise creator.

The central universe, as it was called, was a very old galaxy. All of the molecules and atoms had long been formed together into their loving communities. These clusters, or planets as they are known to you, were the largest that I had ever observed. Some of these groupings of atoms and elements were so massive that they became stars. Oh how gorgeous it was to see them so close. As I was admiring one of these blazing hot communities Red broke by day dream by saying, "See that planet over there?" "I see a great number of planets to be honest," I said. "That one goofy!" she said as she pointed towards one of the smallest of the planets. "Ah yes. Is that the place?" I asked. "That it is," she answered. "Finally," I said. "Let us go then and say hello," I said beginning to approach. "Indeed," she said.

The planet didn't look like much. In fact it looked very much like the Earth's Moon. It was a luminous white color with dark craters peppering its face. As we got closer, Red said to stop. I watched in amazement as the planet turned itself around to face us. The cracks that were in its surface opened to show eyes. A volcano in the center of the planet formed a nose. Some craters stretched open wide into a moaning yawn. After the planet finished his gigantic yawn, he spoke is an old and wise sounding double bass. "I just dreamt that you two were coming to visit me. So strange that the dream came true. Curious things, dreams. Especially when they come true. I created them I still don't understand them." "You are the wise creator?!" I asked in an astonished tone. "Well what did you expect? A wizard in a pointed hat?" he teased. "What is a wizard?" I said utterly confused. "Oh I don't expect you to understand that. They haven't even been created yet," he said. So far, I had no idea what was going on or what this crazy old planet was talking about. "So you have come to ask me where Hate is and how you can defeat him," he said. "Uh," I said nervously as I glanced at Red. "Who am I kidding? Of course you have, BUT I can't give you an answer!" he said. "I cannot! The reason being, I have no clue! I know for a fact that Hate is out there, but I can't see him because he has already made himself a very strong light cloak. Also, I can't tell you how to defeat him because that is the whole point of being able to think right?! So you are going to have to be the one that figures that one out. OR you can just wing it like I do." "I'm sorry, but you are going a little too fast for me. How do we find Hate?" I asked. "Well I can always just send you towards where I last saw him, before he acquired his cloak, and you might be able to find him in that area. That's the thing about

Darks. They are super slow. They lack agility, but they are silent and invisible," he said.

"It is all so…. Overwhelming," I said. "I agree," said Red who had been just floating and listening to the conversation. She continued, "Oh great and wise creator, will you help guide Love to his own realization?" "Well I guess it wouldn't technically be telling him what he has to do…. Why not!" he said. Red and I both took a sigh of relief. The wise creator called me closer and began to teach me how to meditate. Meditation was a very useful tool for me. I found that if I just focused on the movement and vibration of the universe around me I could see in different light spectrums, I could move entire solar systems, and I could feel the slightest feeling of Sadness in the tiniest fish in the tiniest tide pool on Earth from across the universe.

After many many hundreds of thousands of years I had reached a level of strength and maturity so that I was comfortable with even attempting to travel towards Hates location. Before the wise creator pointed us in the right direction Red and I thanked him for helping us. He told us it was his pleasure and his purpose. As we began our long journey to possible destruction, my mind was very much distracted by the question of am I ready. Red had trouble breaking this thought because it was such a great worry in my mind. She saw this so she tried harder and was successful in breaking my trance by saying, "I believe in you and I trust you with all of my being, Love" I couldn't help but smile at her saying this. I didn't know what to say I response, so I just said, "thank you for all that she had done for me, Red." She smiled and said, "You are welcome," and we continued on to kill Hate.

Chapter VI

The route to Hate's last seen location was full of obstacles. There were electromagnetic storms that were the size of galaxies that swept through, destroying all in their paths. Red told me that they were as a result of the negativity of Hate. As we continued, we began to smell something so absolutely rank, that we stopped dead in our tracks. "Goodness! What is that stench?!" I said. "There is a dark nearby," Red exclaimed. "WHAT?! How close is it? Is it Hate? Get behind me so that I can protect you!" "Calm down Love! Just let go of worry and relax. It is not Hate because if it were, we would have already been drawn in by his gravity," Red said comfortingly. I breathed a sigh of relief as I heard her speak. So I began to meditate that way I could see the Dark in ultraviolet light. All of space seemed to slow as I focused on the vibration and motion of the universe. I felt my essence fire out into space. I exited the multiverse and saw all that existed. As I focused even harder

I fell back into my body. I opened my visual organs and saw the Dark, slowly dragging its way through space. I saw all of the poor little photons that were within its grasp.

"Red, we have to do something," I said pitifully. "Do what you must, Love, but be careful. Remember that your true purpose is to destroy Hate. If you get hurt or exhausted, you won't be able to face Hate," she warned. I had already began to move towards the Dark by the time she had finished. As I approached the smell grew stronger. So strong that it was difficult to continue. As I got within the gravitational field of the Dark I noticed that it had noticed me and was beginning to turn towards me. It began to speak as I was drawn more near. "Ah! Lunch is early today! I shall enjoy feasting on your mass," it mocked. "Lucky for me, I have no mass you smelly Dark," I said as my face contorted from the smell. "Well I will just add you to my cloak, so that I can hear you squeal from my smell." As the Dark finished his sentence, I heard all of the photons that were trapped shriek. They screamed for me to escape while I still could. "Don't worry my sweets, I can handle this little moon of a Dark," I said.

I looked at the Dark one last time before I began to meditate again. I again felt my essence fire out of the multiverse and fall back to my body. But when I opened my eyes, nothing had changed. The Dark was still pulling me in. I began to panic and move about, trying to escape the inescapable grasp. Red started to move closer to help but I said, "No Red! It was my mistake. Don't drag yourself in too." She understood and stayed away. I moved faster and faster towards the Dark. He began to chuckle at my stupidity. "You practically gave yourself to me, you fool!" It mocked once again. I was completely overwhelmed. I thought about how I would never see Red again. I thought about how I would miss the beautiful sight of Grins, popping in and out of existence. I thought of Hate devouring the entire multiverse. I began to cry as I disappeared into darkness.

Red began to cry as well as she saw me disappear. She slowly turned away as the photons surrounding the Dark began to scream again. She stopped to listen to them. She turned to listen more closely as she realized that the photons were not screaming. They were cheering! She watched as the Dark began to swell and contract a million times a second. Its expanding and contracting became more significant until the Dark completely collapsed into a tiny little star. No bigger than a moon. All of the photons that were trapped rushed in towards the center as if to celebrate. Red quickly followed them.

As Red approached, she saw me glowing from all of the photons hugging me and thanking me for helping them. "Hi Red," I said. She didn't know what to say, so she just smiled and embraced me. All of the photons left together in a beam of light into the vastness of space.

"What… How… How did you do that?" Red asked, dumbfounded. "I just thought of how much I loved you Red. I started to cry because I thought I would never see you again. I guess my tears made that dark feel me and it decided to let go of all its mass out of guilt, and go back to being a star," I said. She looked at me and smiled again. We moved over to the former Dark and confronted it. It turned out that it was a she. She apologized sincerely and said that we had the right to take her to the Wise creator for punishment. We told her that she was forgiven and I gave her another tear to comfort her, for she was feeling extraordinarily guilty.

We left the now loving star to begin a new life of warming a solar system of tiny new planets that formed from all of the released mass. The planets formed life and became one of the healthiest and happiest solar systems in the universe. As for Red and I, we continued on to find Hate, for our journey had just begun. I learned a great deal from confronting that first Dark. I made it my duty from then on that I would use my power to liberate every single Dark that I came into contact with.

I confronted many more Darks on our way to Hate. All were challenging. They all had hidden weapons and they all had a taste for eating things, but I was glad to help them with their eating disorder. I was kind of like a personal trainer on your planet. Coaching their clients into a smaller pants size. Except I cried into their mouths and they exploded. Now that I think about it, I was very different from a fitness trainer. That was a dumb comparison on my part. Anyway, we continued on our journey as I grew in wisdom and experiences of liberating Darks.

Chapter VII

The strain of the entire universe rested on my shoulders. The destiny that had been dropped into my lap was unreal. I felt like the future of infinity had been entrusted with such an inexperienced child. I felt as though I was treading water while having to hold a paralyzed whale above the surface so that it didn't drown. Although so many thoughts of doubt ran through my brain, I still felt that somehow, I would make it. I felt as though someone had my back. Someone was looking out for me.

As we flew through space at unbelievable speeds, we came within five hundred light years of Hate. Neither of us could see him, for Hate's light cloak was too strong, but I could feel the suffering that was taking place. As we passed a cold and lonely planet in the middle of deep nothingness, we decided to take a short rest. I looked at the planet and thought, 'poor little planet. He has no one to Love.' I said to Red, "I wish there was something that I could do to make that planet less lonely." "So do I, dear," she said. "Well maybe there is something I could do," I said as I remembered how much I changed Earth by giving myself to her. I slowly moved toward the planet. I looked deep into the planet's heart and saw a glimmer of Hope. Hope that someone would come along and give it company.

At the sight of this hope I began to do something that I had never tried to do before. I tried to create. I thought, 'If the wise creator can do it, why can't I,' so, I began to meditate. I zoomed out and in, then I pictured in my mind's eye a moon. A moon to keep the lonely planet company. But because this planet was so cold, I had to make the moon hot, that way it could keep the planet warm as well. When I saw in my mind how happy both of the celestial beings where, I cried at how beautiful they were together. I opened my eyes in astonishment as I gazed upon the prettiest little companionship. My tears had made the moon and its warmth. The warmth of the moon caused the frozen oceans and soil on the cold planet to thaw, giving way to lush forests. I smiled at how both bodies gave each other what they needed. The planet needed warmth and company, while the moon needed company and a beautiful view. I left the two love birds so that they could introduce themselves. Pure beauty was my business and it made me happy.

I felt the suffering as a human feels the waves rush over them as they sit on the ocean shore. The feeling of being completely overcome and then dragged with the reseeding wave as it returns to its master.

Near silence grew in my mind as we traveled along. The absence of thought in my mind made time seem to pass by much slower. I was overwhelmed by all that was around me. I saw the beauty of a star in the distance. I heard and felt the vibration of screaming photons. I could smell a faint hint of the ripe odor of Hate. But what overwhelmed me the most is how when I glanced over at Red I couldn't help but think that I shouldn't drag her into it for fear of her being trapped if I fail.

I urged for us to stop one last time before our final approach of Hate, so we did. "Red?" I said, "I fear that if you come any further, that harm will befall you if I fail." "What are you saying?" she asked. "I don't want to be responsible for harm that may come to you if I fail." I said. "Love," Red said in the most soothing motherly voice, "Whatever happens, happens and we have little to no control over it. All I know is that I am definitely not leaving your side. Not ever in a million years my sweet and humble Love." She spoke with comparison to a mother that uses her sweet whispered voice to silence a baby as it begins to fuss. I gave her a worried look but I knew that there was no use in trying to persuade her. So, I told her that I was ready to finish this. And so we moved along to destroy the smelly monster known as Hate. Though we were both very worried, we didn't say, in fear of worrying one another. Therefore, we remained silent.

Chapter VIII

There he was. Hate. The essence of pure and utter torture. The soul of absolute destruction. The devil. The enemy. What is the enemy of love? I did not know. As a human you would say that such a thing does not exist. To something that has never felt or seen what love has to offer, I would be the most dangerous enemy. I see now that it is similar to that which humans do on their planet. I have seen that humans are absolutely terrified by something that they don't know much about.

So many stories are told on Earth about conquering foreign land and killing that which lived there before. The true reason for this is not conquest or for civilization. It is because of the "heathens". The mindless and different. Something that you cannot control scares you. And I think that because neither I nor Hate could control one another, we both had a sense of fear, or caution about us as we met.

"Hello friend," I said. Hate responded with a hiss and a growl, "I have felt you approaching for a long time Love." "I have felt you as well, Hate," I countered. "Are you the only thing that that old and cold rock, the creator, has sent to destroy me? What a pity," he mocked. "Why do you feud with me brother?" I asked, "We don't need to argue or throw insults like stones in a pond. The only thing that will come from it is ripples that will be felt for infinity." "Don't speak down to me! You are but a child! I do not know you, but I do know that you are not my friend or my brother. So leave or I will breathe you and your little photon in like a nebula of helium gas," Hate fumed. "I beg you. Please let the photons go and feel what I have to give. You will not regret it," I pleaded. "No! Now that you will not leave I shall consume you," Hate said as he moved towards us and we both nudged forward like being locked in the stream of solar wind from a fading star.

In a panic I closed my eyes and instantly visualized Red back with the wise creator but when I opened my eyes she was still right next to me, looking at me with the a hopeless look of absolute fear. I could not meditate for too much fear had swelled up in my mind. It shrouded my mind like how a dense layer of fog slithers through the trees on a quiet moist morning on Earth. As we reached the horizon line of Hate, I reached out to touch Red one last time. She was just out of my grasp. She stayed trapped with all of the other photons, on the horizon, as I fell deeper and deeper into the mouth of the terrible beast known as Hate.

I felt my mortal vessel collapse one million times as I fell. The pain was so great that I cried out. I couldn't help it. What could I do? The fog grew even denser in my mind. It felt as though it turned to acid that was on fire. I felt my body reach the singularity. I closed my eyes, even though it was too dark to see, and I accepted my inevitable fate.

I opened my eyes to see a nebula. The birth place of all that has been. I saw Hate as a child. I saw him smile upon the most beautiful family of planets. I saw him warm them and cherish them with all of his being. The time sped forward and I saw as one by one each of the planets grew so close to Hate that he burned them to nothingness. I saw that Hate didn't understand why he couldn't touch them. He tried again and again until all but one was left. In order to save his last friend Hate flung him into empty space. Hate became so sad that he had killed all that he found beautiful in the universe. So sad in fact that he died inside. He fell in on himself under his strain and became what he was. An evil, misguided, terror of the universe.

Everything went black except for a faint pin hole of light. The light grew larger, as if I was exiting a tunnel. The light completely consumed me and I saw the entire multiverse. I saw it all. I saw everything from the smallest grain of sand on Earth to back of my own head. I saw that everything that ever existed or ever will exist thriving in a single drop of rain that fell from a cloud. I saw the raindrop that was my universe splatter against a blade of grass. I turned around and noticed all of the emotions standing behind me. Watching me. Speaking to each other about me. They stood there left to right: Happiness, Sadness, Excitement, Dread, Anger, Tranquility, Fear, and Hope. They moved into a circle around me. They spoke in one voice. All united into one mind.

"We have been waiting for a long time, Love, for you to let go. To let go of your mortal self and join us in the outer realm," they said in a monotone alien voice. "Where am I?" I enquired. "Where is Red? Why is the universe in a rain drop? Why did the entire universe just splatter into nothing against that blade of grass?" "Be at peace," they said "that was just one of the many infinite copies of our universe that is created for every single decision someone or something makes in the universe. Each frame in our universe is just another droplet that falls. By the time that it hits that leaf, everything has already been transferred to another drop. So, do not fear for those you care about," They reassured.

"I want to go back to Red! Send me back!" I demanded. "We alone cannot send you back," they said, "but, there is a way that is theorized. We could converge. Then and only then will we have enough strength and power to move the multiverse." "So be it," I said. They closed in around me and in a bright flash we converged. I felt all that the others had to offer. Good and bad. Through all of these feelings and emotions I felt strength. I felt wisdom. I felt keen and sharp. I closed my eyes and the rest of me followed suit. We visualized ourselves back in my mortal body. We visualized floating in space alongside Hate. As we opened our eyes, it was so.

We said aloud, "Hate, you of all know that you cannot kill that which you know too little about." Hate turned to us and rushed towards us with all of his force as he screamed. We held our ground as both bodies collided.

Chapter IX

The collision sent ripples though the time plane. They were felt by the Wise Creator, by Earth, and every single molecule I had shared myself with. They all knew that the most important battle in the history of the universe was underway. The Earth cried and flooded her surface. The Wise Creator closed his eyes and meditated. The Grins continued to flash in and out of existence. The dark lonely planet embraced his darling moon. All whom I had touched, worried for me, but at the same time trusted in me. Therefore, they had a sense of peace.

All was still and dark as Hate hit our union of emotion. Time seamed to stop and take a breath. As it slowly began to resume, a brilliant flash of light shone like a lighthouse beam across the universe. It shone so bright, and so long, that it burst the multiverse bubble and we were forced to jump to another.

After jumping, the light faded into an explosion. The explosion we saw was made up of every single molecule of gas, dust, star, galaxy, or photon that Hate had ever consumed. The blast was so powerful that it ripped our emotional union apart so that I had my body, but all of the other emotions were just suspended spirits.

Similar to the initial beam of light, the blinding and tearing explosion faded. Steam and dust froze in place as the area around us cooled to its normal temperature. I couldn't see Hate. In fear that I had completely destroyed him, I began to move the frozen beads of ice and dust out of the way so that I could try to find him. I began to see a slight red glow through the clutter. I moved one last layer of debris out of my way. Then I saw something that I did not expect. I saw Red. My mother. My darling photon. But something was different about her. She was so still that she changed her color to a sub-red color. It had seemed as though she had mode a circle through the color spectrum. As she turned to face me, I could see that she held a child. A tiny shinning white star that was the size of a grain of sand. She looked up at me and said, "Quiet Love. He is sleeping." "What happened?" I asked. "He was only a troubled soul. He was the saddest little thing I had ever met. You saw his past didn't you?" she said. "I did, but how are you here?" I asked.

"I panicked after I saw you disappear into his belly, so I got all of the other photons to push their way right in after you but I couldn't quite reach you in time." She said. "I saw you completely vanish out of existence and in your place I saw a glimmer of this little guy. A sweet memory. A sweet little glimmer of you. Love! In all of that

Hate there was true Love! I touched the little glimmer and I saw Hates past. Just as Hate pulled all of the photons back out of his belly I held on to this glimmer."

"How could I exist within Hate?! How could I exist before I existed?!" I asked. "Can't you see?! You are an Emotion. You were never made. You were never born. You just move in a cycle. You live in the outer realm until you are needed here. Then, you are born again in order to change the universe. There is always a balance. There must be. Too much Sadness gives birth to Happiness. Too much Excitement gives birth to Dread. Too much Anger gives birth to Tranquility. Too much Fear gives birth to Hope. When Hate is too strong, Love will come to equalize the imbalance," She said.

At about this time the tiny glimmer of me awoke. They looked into my very soul and began to expand quite quickly until he stopped at about the size of an asteroid. He opened his mouth and let out a little black rock. That little black rock was the core of Hate. The glimmer of me had protected him from any harm. As the rock floated peacefully toward us, the other emotions moved into a circle around him. They all looked at me and spoke in one voice. "Thank you Love for all that you have done to return balance to the universe." I nodded at them and they disappeared to the outer realm. They took Hate with them, leaving behind an empty shell that was the tiny black rock. The glimmer of me shrank back down to its original size and then faded to nothingness right before our eyes.

Words cannot explain how I felt in that moment. Just thinking of it now makes me shiver. I turned to Red and cried. I embraced her and cried into her. She glowed brighter as my tears met he nucleus. We broke our embrace and began to travel back towards the Wise Creator.

Chapter X

Our return journey seemed to take much less time than it had before. All along the way we were greeted by every solar system and nebula with fanfare. It didn't seem very right to me. It felt as if it had ended so quickly. It felt like all that I did was only in the name of what was right. In my mind that doesn't require any reward.

We stopped by old friends that we had made along our initial journey but they all treated us as if they didn't know us. We tried to travel slower so that we could truly enjoy the time together, Red and I. it seemed as though we hadn't ever talked without a silent whisper in the back of our minds telling us that we might not make it through our journey. Now that all of our worries were over and done with, we could breath. We could have normal conversations without worry of the future. We laughed, we cried, and we cherished all that we had.

As we came closer to the Central Galaxy we felt unsure. We felt as though we wouldn't be together much longer. We entered into the outer edges of the Central Galaxy. I stopped and turned to Red. "Thank you, Red, for all that you have done for me. All that you have taught me and all that you've showed me. I couldn't have asked for a more faithful and caring companion on my voyage," I said. "My darling Love, I have had the time of my existence. You have showed me the true meaning of the universe. You have given me all that any little photon like me could ask for. I am the one that should be thanking you," she responded.

We continued into the middle of the galaxy. We greeted the Wise Creator. I could see that there was something on his mind. Something that made him hesitant to be joyful and silly like he usually was.

"What is the matter?" I asked him. "You are looking quite grim." He responded by saying, "Oh dear boy, I wish I had better news than that which I have to say. I know that you are happy now that Hate has transcended to the outer realm and you are free of worry, but nothing lasts forever." "What are you saying?" Red interrupted. "Well," he said nervously, "Love, you have to move on. Now that you have returned balance to the universe you must return to your true self and existence in the outer realm."

My heart sank when I heard these words. I knew that this was coming. It's almost like I heard the universe whisper it in my ear, warning me about it before hand, but I chose to ignore it. Never the less I chose to accept my fate. I turned to Red and didn't say a word.

Instead I gave her a single tear and a single embrace. I turned to The Wise Creator and he asked, "Now, the way this works is, before I dematerialize you, you get to choose what you can leave behind in order to spread your essence on after you leave. What will it be kid?" I thought for a moment and looked at Red. "This," I said as I gave Red a kiss. "Very well then," he said. "So be it."

I felt the same feeling that I had while I passed on inside of Hate. The same white dot that turned into the tunnel, consuming me. I saw the drop of water fall and hit the leaf. I knew that I had completed my purpose. I knew that all was well as I joined my kin in the outer realm.

I shall end at the beginning. Of all the places in between that and infinity, the beginning seems the best to end with. Never forget, human, that all things that you will ever know and ever have known are infinite. Infinite to the infinite degree. From the cells in your mind that allowed you to read this story, to the kiss that you give to your mother when you wake up in the morning. More than anything else, Love is infinite, but I can only begin my infinity if you take me into your soul and embrace me with your essence. Never let me go, and never let any harm befall that which you share me with. Now, go on and live your life. Live it without any Sadness, Dread, Anger, Fear, or Hate. I know that we never have control over these things.

So, remember that Happiness, Excitement, Tranquility, Hope, and most importantly Love will be there to bring your life to balance again.

The End

Printed in Great Britain
by Amazon